BALLROOM BONANZA

Concept and Illustrations by

Nina Rycroft

Story by

Nina Rycroft AND Stephen Harris

Abrams Books for Young Readers

London

In the famous town of Blackpool,
Each October, you will find
Gathered in the Tower Ballroom
Animals of every kind.

It's a dancing competition.
Who will win the prize this year?
Let us watch as keen contenders
Alphabetically appear.

A a First, the affluent alpacas
All arrive, superbly dressed.

B b Then the bears in bright boleros.
(Everyone is most impressed.)

Cc On the floor the camels conga
In the latest Latin style.

Dd Donkeys demonstrate the disco.
    (This can last for quite a while.)

E e Elephants like belly-dancing,
Entertaining all their friends—
Watch their bellies wibble-wobble
Even when the music ends.

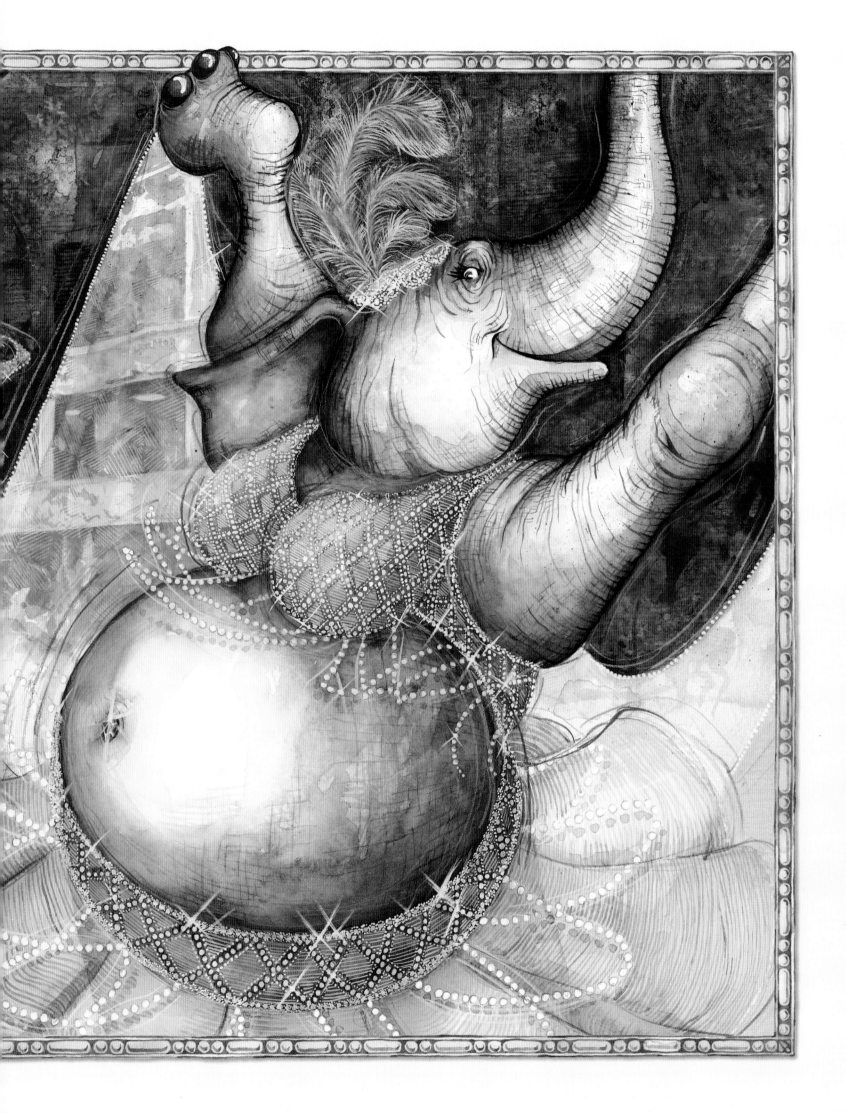

F f | When flamingos dance flamenco,
Judges have to block their ears.

G g Groovy goats try go-go dancing.
(No one's laughed as much in years.)

H h
Here we have the hefty hippos.
Happily their hooves they pound,
Heaving to the latest hip-hop
With their hats the wrong way round.

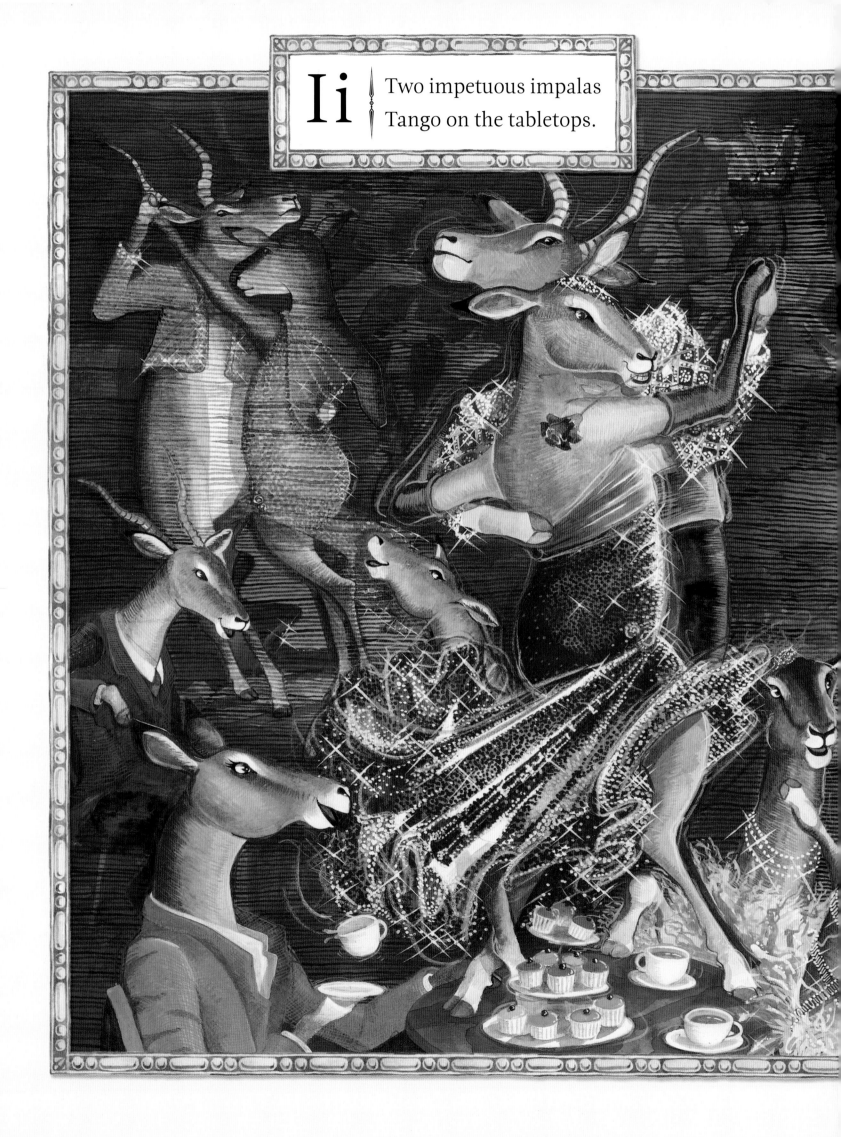

I i

Two impetuous impalas
Tango on the tabletops.

Jj Next, a jaguar who jetés
Blushes as her tutu drops.

Kk Kangaroos are keen on cancan—
Such a night they'd never miss.

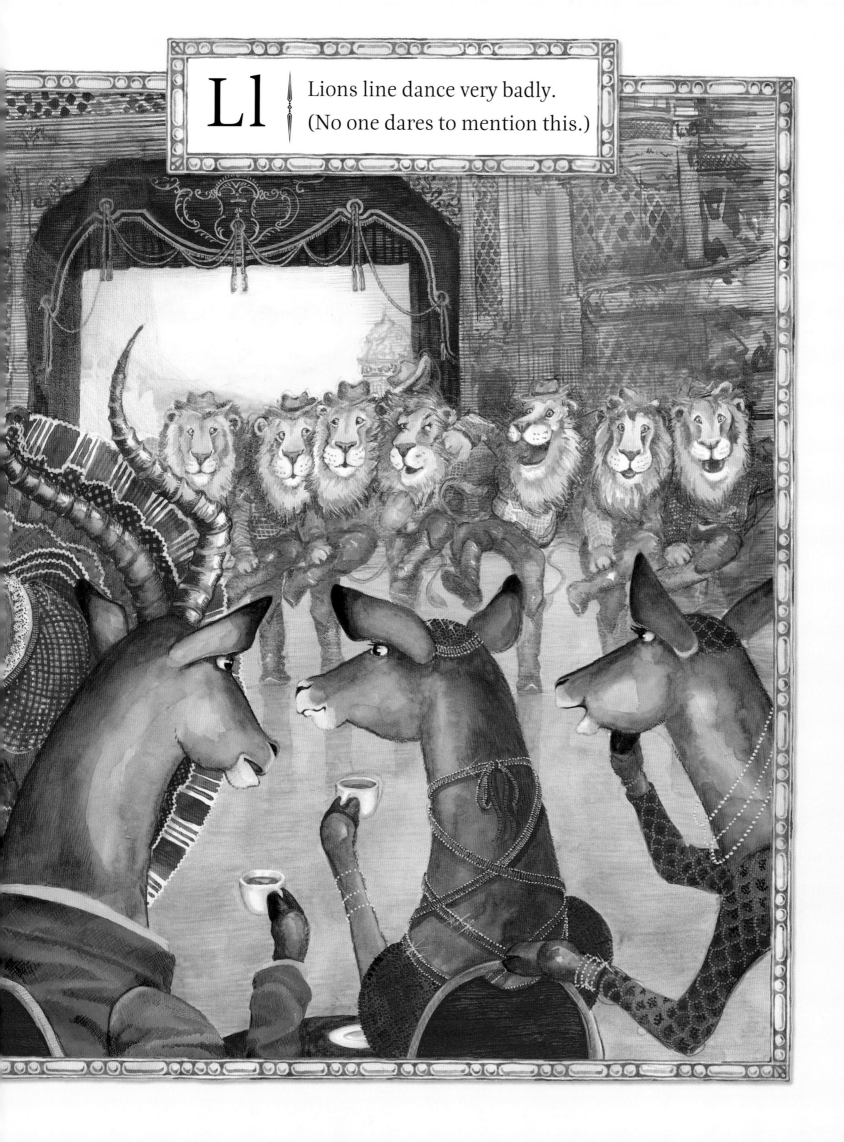

Ll

Lions line dance very badly.
(No one dares to mention this.)

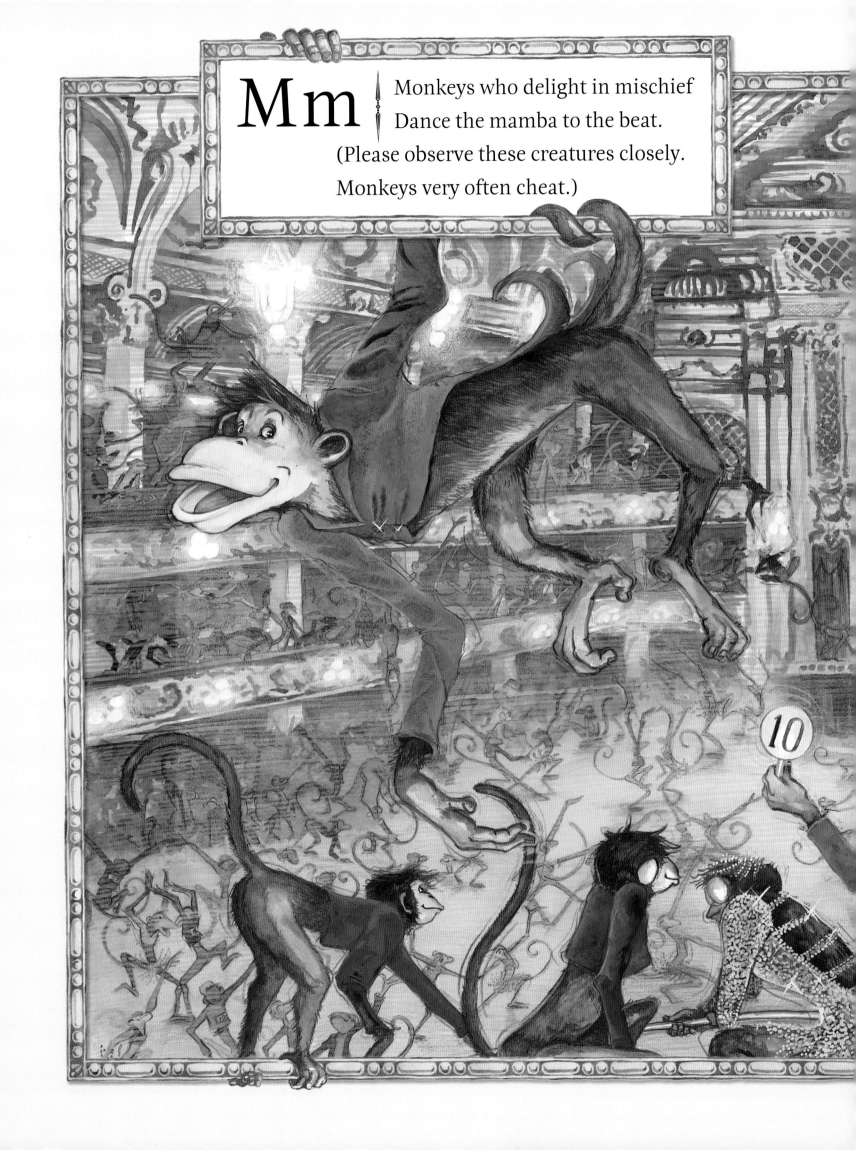

Mm

Monkeys who delight in mischief
Dance the mamba to the beat.
(Please observe these creatures closely.
Monkeys very often cheat.)

Numbats nimbly do the Nutbush
(Not a clever dance, it's true).

O o Followed by orangutans
Who bop and do the boogaloo.

P p Penguins proudly take their partners,
Then the polka they present.

Q q | Quails dance a quaint quadrille
And question where those monkeys went.

R r When the rhinos do the rumba,
No one can believe their eyes.
Hardly anything is broken,
Much to everyone's surprise.

S s Sassy swans perform the samba,
Shaking tail feathers white.

T t Turkeys do the twist, and ponder
What the monkeys plan tonight.

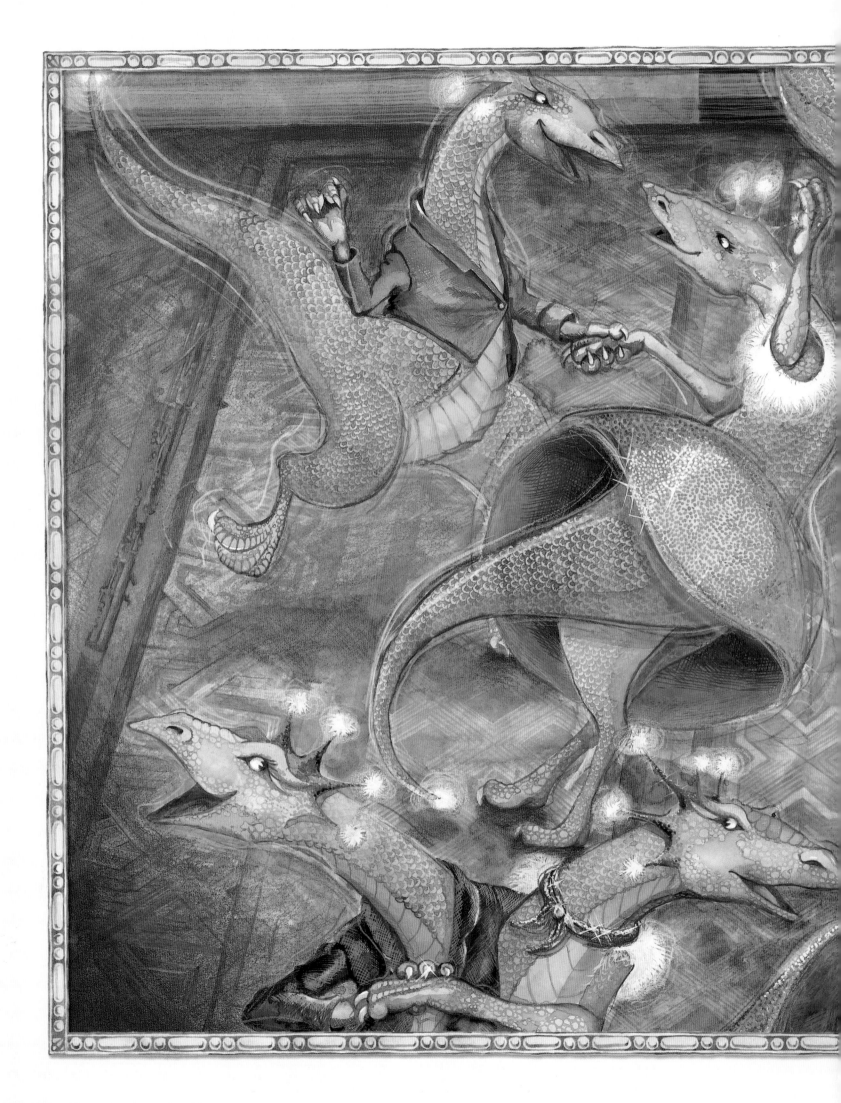

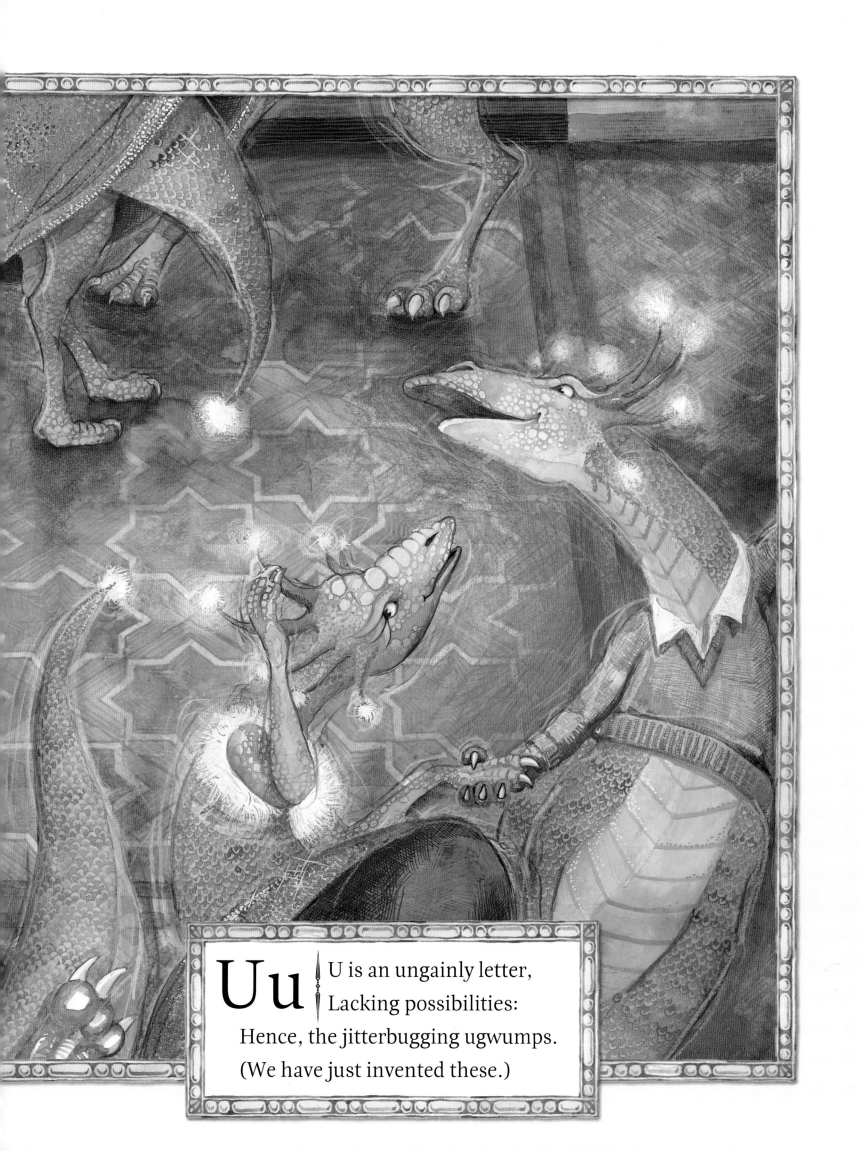

Uu U is an ungainly letter,
Lacking possibilities:
Hence, the jitterbugging ugwumps.
(We have just invented these.)

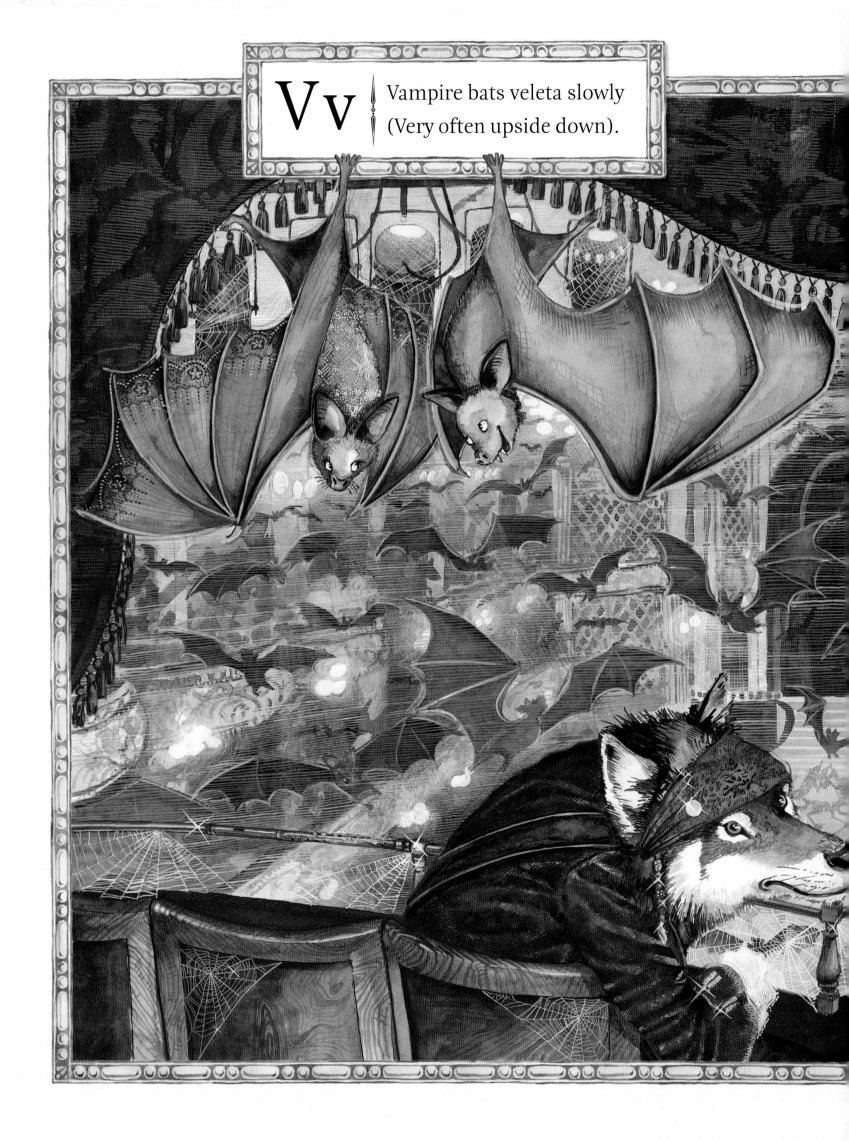

V v

Vampire bats veleta slowly
(Very often upside down).

W w Wolves and wolverines watusi,
Wailing till they wake the town.

Xx Oxen foxtrot extra-quickly—
Such an excellent display!

Yy Yaks enjoy the hootchy-kootchy
In a hurly-burly kind of way.

Zz Last of all, we have the zebras,
Putting on a ritzy show.
They can dance the zapateado.
(No one can pronounce it, though.)

Judges try to pick a winner
In a manner just and fair.
Finding that it's far from easy,
"All are winners!" they declare.

After that, the grand finale.
Dancers ask the band to play.
"Sorry, but those naughty monkeys
Hid our instruments!" they say.

Check each page from A to Z, now.
Prove you're good at monkey tricks!
Find the hidden instruments.
(In total, there are twenty-six.)

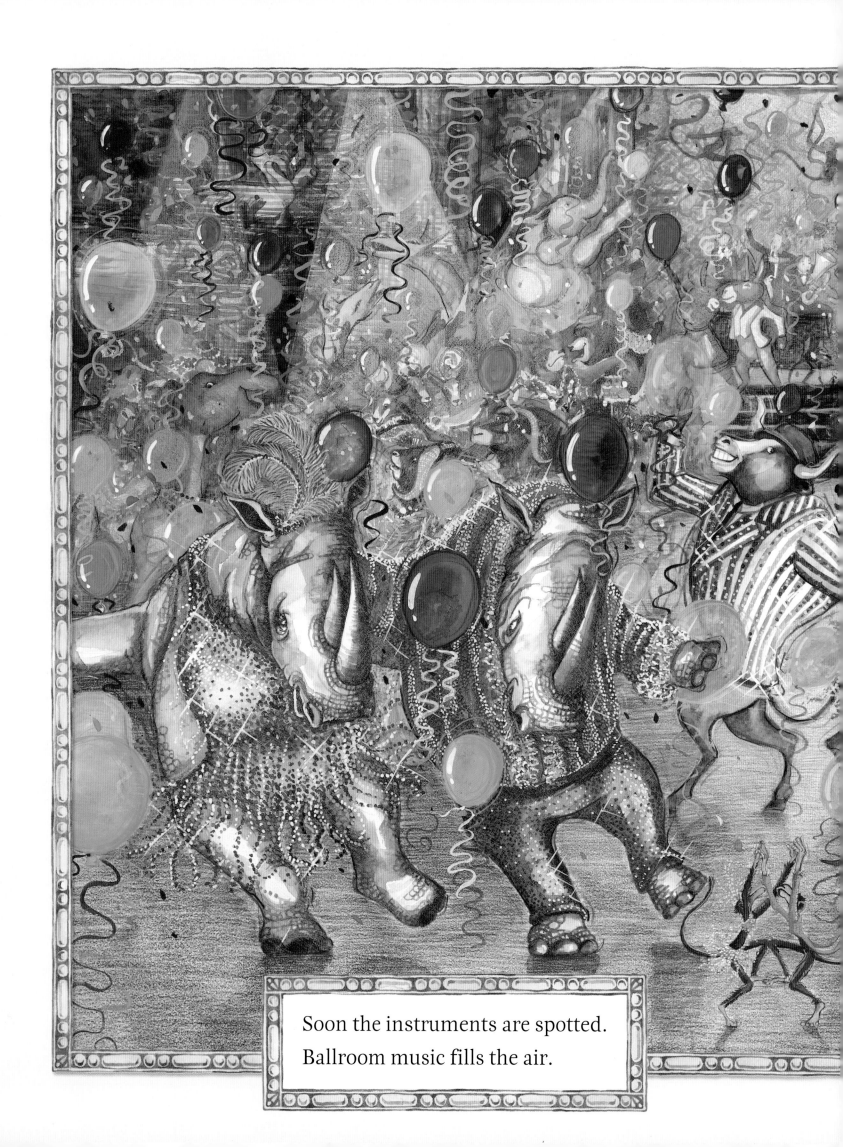

Soon the instruments are spotted.
Ballroom music fills the air.

Jiving, flinging, stomping, swinging
Animals are everywhere.

Dreamily they leave the ballroom
Just as dawn is drawing near.
Everybody makes a promise:
"See you all again next year."